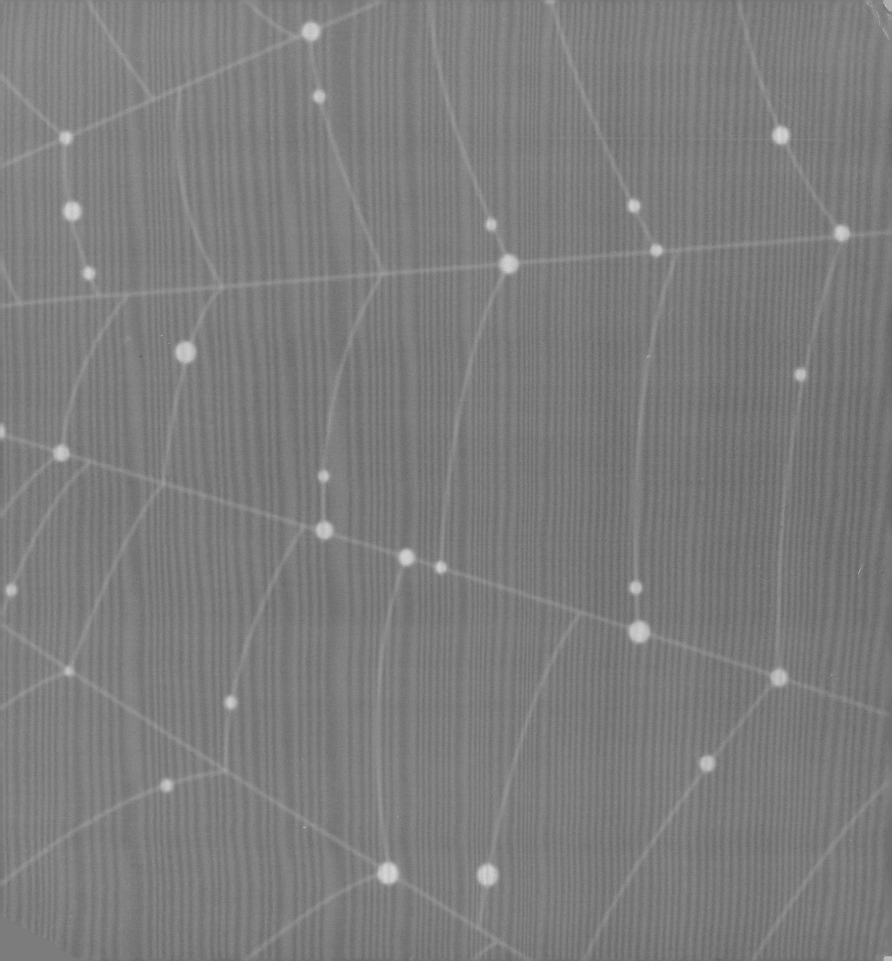

Published by Top That! Publishing plc
Tide Mill Way, Woodbridge, Suffolk, IP12 1AP, UK
www.topthatpublishing.com
Illustration copyright © Top That! Publishing plc 2011
Text copyright © June Morley 2011
All rights reserved
0 2 4 6 8 9 7 5 3 1
Printed and bound in China

Creative Director – Simon Couchman
Editorial Director – Daniel Graham

Written by June Morley
Illustrated by Marina Le Ray

ISBN 978-1-84956-439-7

A catalogue record for this book is available from the British Library
Printed and bound in China

TIME FOR DINNER

Written by June Morley
Illustrated by Marina Le Ray

For my mum, Audrey Carter - JM

Spider stopped spinning her sticky web.
'I'm hungry,' she said ... 'Time for dinner.'

Just then, a big fly buzzed
around and around the tree.

'Yum, yum,' said Spider.
'He looks nice and juicy.'

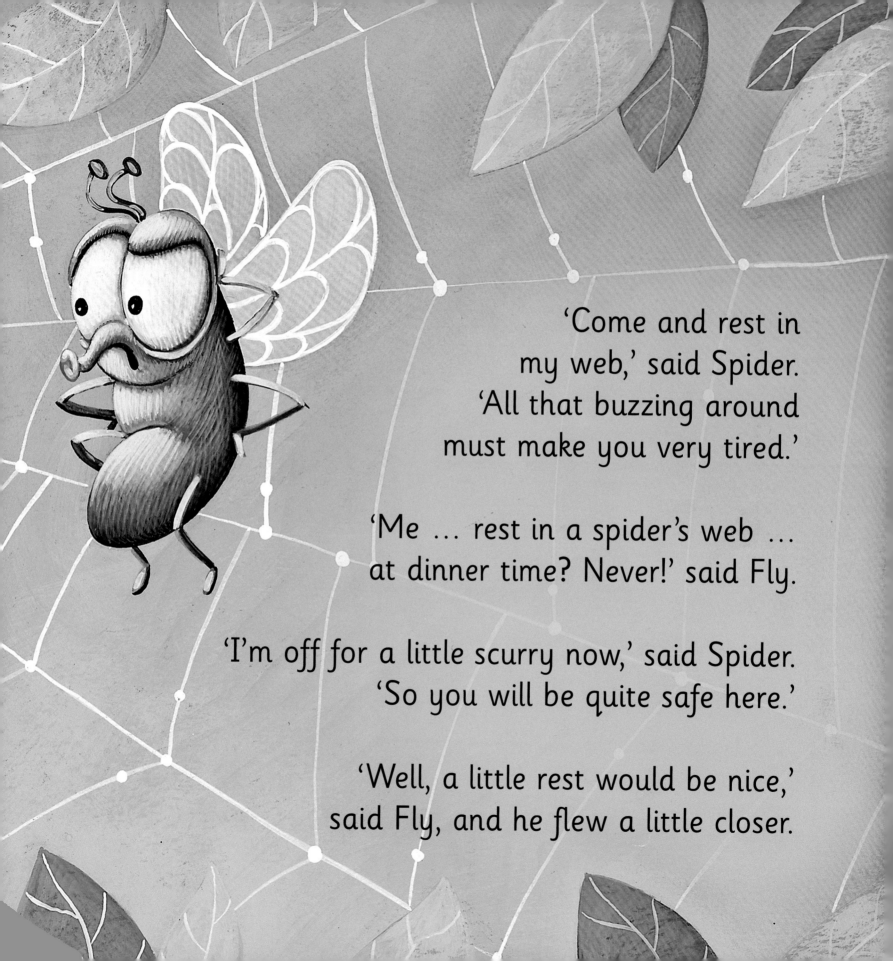

'Come and rest in
my web,' said Spider.
'All that buzzing around
must make you very tired.'

'Me ... rest in a spider's web ...
at dinner time? Never!' said Fly.

'I'm off for a little scurry now,' said Spider.
'So you will be quite safe here.'

'Well, a little rest would be nice,'
said Fly, and he flew a little closer.

Bird stopped tidying her nest.
'I'm hungry,' she said ... 'Time for dinner.'

Just then, Spider came scurrying up the tree.

'Yum, yum,' said Bird. 'Come and rest in my nest. All that scurrying must make you very tired.'

'Me ... rest in a bird's nest ... at dinner time?
Never!' said Spider.

'I'm off for a little flutter now,' said Bird.
'So you will be quite safe here.'

'Well, a little rest would be nice,'
said Spider, and she drew a little closer.

Fluffy Cat stopped rolling on his mat.
'I'm hungry,' he said … 'Time for dinner.'

Just then, Bird came fluttering down.

'Yum, yum … she looks nice and plump,'
said Fluffy Cat.

'Come and rest on my mat,'
said Fluffy Cat. 'All that fluttering
must make you very tired.'

'Me ... rest on a cat's mat ... at dinner time?
Never!' said Bird.

'I'm off for a little snooze now,' said Fluffy Cat.
'So you will be quite safe here.'

Then Fluffy Cat sneaked off under a bush and waited.

'Fluffy Cat must be fast asleep now,' said Bird,
and she fluttered down onto the mat.

'Time for dinner,' said Fluffy Cat,
and he crept out from the bush.

Shaggy Dog saw Fluffy Cat and
stopped chewing his bone.

'WOOF ... WOOF,' barked Shaggy Dog,
which frightened Fluffy Cat.

He leapt high in the air!

WOOF
WOOF

'MIAOW ... MIAOW,'
screeched Fluffy Cat,
which frightened Bird.

She flapped her wings hard and
flew to the top of the tree.

'SQUAWK ... SQUAWK,'
screeched Bird,
which frightened Spider.

'I'm off,' said Spider,
and she scurried all the
way back to her web.

'Time for dinner,' she said.

But Fly wasn't in Spider's web and he wasn't buzzing around the tree.

Fly was busy nibbling Shaggy Dog's bone.

'Yum, yum,' said Fly.
'I do love dinner time!'